This Book Belongs To:

Library of Congress Cataloging-in-Publication Data

McLean, Michael, 1952–

   The forgotten carols : a Christmas miracle for Isaac and Eliza / Michael McLean ; illustrated by Brandon Dorman.

      p. cm.

   Summary: An extraordinary visitor brings a miracle to the Christmas season of Isaac and Eliza Rose, two young children who lost their father the year before.

   ISBN 978-1-60641-844-4 (hardbound : alk. paper)

   [1. Single-parent families—Fiction. 2. Brothers and sisters—Fiction. 3. Babysitters—Fiction.

   4. Jesus Christ—Nativity—Fiction. 5. Christmas—Fiction. 6. Carols—Fiction.] I. Dorman, Brandon, ill. II. Title.

   PZ7.M4786995For 2010

   [Fic]—dc22

                                      2010026788

Printed in the United States of America

Inland Graphics, Menomonee Falls, WI

10 9 8 7 6 5 4 3 2 1

THE FORGOTTEN CAROLS

A CHRISTMAS MIRACLE FOR ISAAC AND ELIZA

Written and narrated by
※ **MICHAEL McLEAN** ※
with illustrations by Brandon Dorman

DESERET
BOOK

SALT LAKE CITY, UTAH

Most people love Christmas. But not Isaac and Eliza Rose! Their dad, Captain Rose, had courageously given his life last Christmas, fighting for freedom in a land far away. Christmas this year seemed sad and empty without him. The best they could do was pretend to be excited about the holiday.

When Isaac and Eliza's mom brought home a fresh pine wreath, they knew she was pretending too. "I'm sorry it's not a tree," she apologized, "but I thought maybe the smell of the pine needles would make it feel more like Christmas around here, anyway." The children didn't think it helped much.

On Christmas Eve, Mom snuggled between Isaac and Eliza on the couch and read them *The Night before Christmas.* Even that tradition didn't feel quite right. And things got even worse when Mom said softly, "Children, I have to work the late shift again tonight."

"Ohhhh," the children groaned. "But Mom, we want you with us."

"Now, don't you worry," said their mother. "I met a lovely, interesting woman who works in the maternity ward of the hospital. When she heard I needed someone to stay with my kids tonight, she volunteered—on two conditions: that we hadn't decorated our tree yet, and that she could bring something for dinner. I told her that we didn't even have a tree, and that I hadn't made supper plans. How could I not like this lady? I hope you will too."

When the Mystery Sitter arrived, she was lugging a backpack about the size of a kitchen garbage can with a green Christmas tree painted on it. It looked really strange seeing a woman that old with a backpack that big, but for some reason she didn't seem weird to Isaac and Eliza. They liked how she smiled and winked at them as she waved their mother out the door. Then she turned and clapped her hands together, her eyes twinkling.

First, the cocoa," the sitter announced. She pulled a thermos out of her backpack and filled three cups to the brim with steaming hot chocolate. "To the unexpected miracles of Christmas!" she toasted, raising her cup. She took a sip and nodded to the children to do the same. "Are you ready?" she asked.

Isaac and Eliza exchanged confused looks.

The woman laughed. "Well, of course you can't answer that. How could anyone know if they're ready for something unexpected? Silly me." And then, from deep in her backpack, she pulled a leather case that seemed to have light spilling out of the creases and cracks. She opened the case and took out what looked like a handmade Christmas ornament. It was shaped like some kind of building. Passing it to Isaac, she said, "Put this inn on the tree first, and we'll wait for the miracle."

B ut we don't have a tree," Isaac pointed out.

"Of course you don't." She laughed at herself again. "Your mother told me that. But that wreath will do." She gently nudged Isaac and the ornament he was holding toward the wreath above the fireplace mantel. He placed the ornament on one of the lower branches and sat down. Nothing happened.

"We can't rush this. Miracles are funny that way," said the woman. "They happen when they happen." She took another sip of her cocoa and motioned to the children to do the same.

And there they sat, sipping and waiting. Sipping and waiting. Sipping and waiting.

When the chocolate was all but gone, the furniture seemed to rumble just a bit, and a whiff of exotic spices blew gently through the room. Suddenly a man stood before them, dressed in clothing that looked like the robes Isaac and Eliza had seen on the figures in their grandmother's Nativity set. He walked toward the little inn-shaped ornament resting on the lower branch of the wreath, touched it for a moment, and smiled. And then, before Isaac could ask his name, he started to sing about a very special Bethlehem night:

THE INNKEEPER
(LET HIM IN)

I am a man forgotten;
 no one recalls my name.
Thousands of years will fail to fully
 erase my shame.
But I turned a profit nicely that day
That I turned the couple away…
 I turned them away.

I didn't sleep that evening,
 though I'd sold out my place.
Somehow I felt uneasy…
 something about her face.
Why did I wish that I'd let
 them stay?
I don't think they could have paid…
 or could they have paid?

Restless I left my bedroom,
 I walked the streets all night,
Lost in the world I lived in.
Found by a heavenly light.

And I knew where the cry had come
 from
'Cause I'd told them where they
 could go,
But I didn't think I could face them,
So I walked slowly home,
Missing my chance to share
 in their joy.
I never saw the boy.

He never would condemn me.
I did that all on my own.
He offered His forgiveness,
And ever since then I've known
He lets us choose each hour of
 each day,
If we'll let Him in to stay.

Let Him in… let Him in…
 let the hope and joy begin.
Let Him in… let Him in…
 let the peace on earth begin.
Whether it be in your world today
Or a crowded Bethlehem inn,
Find a way… make Him room…
 let Him in.

The song ended, and the man disappeared as quickly as he had come.

"More cocoa, children?" the sitter offered cheerfully. "If it's all right with you, I'll have another cup." She looked at Isaac and Eliza and smiled. "Don't feel like you have to say anything. First time with a Christmas miracle usually leaves people a bit speechless."

She reached into the leather case and drew out another object. "Here, Eliza. Your turn. Put this on the wreath." She handed Isaac's sister an ornament that looked like an ancient flute.

Before Eliza got the flute even halfway to the wreath, she was met by a young shepherd boy who asked her if he could examine the ornament.

"My, this looks like a little version of my flute," said the boy. "I used it to play my flock to sleep at night. Problem was, the music I made was so soothing that it put me to sleep faster than my sheep. That's why I missed the big night. I slept through the whole thing." Distant music began to play, and the boy began to sing.

THE SHEPHERD
(YOU WERE NOT THERE
IN BETHLEHEM)

The flock was more than peaceful.
The night was dark and deep.
The stillness wrapped around me,
I drifted off to sleep.
And when my friends awoke me,
Oh, what a tale they had to tell!

They said the angels told them
About a newborn king.
They had a star to guide them.
They heard the heavens sing.
They said that when they found Him,
They knew they'd never be the same.

Somehow I did believe them
Though everything I knew said
   I should not believe them.
This story can't be true.
But there was something magic
   in the air
That made me feel as if I had
   been there.

I asked a thousand questions.
Their answers startled me.
The more I heard, the more I thought
I knew this could not be.
And then the struggle started—
My head was wrestling with
   my heart.
Why would a God from heaven

Come to the world this way?
Why in a lowly stable
Would the Messiah lay?
I shook my head and asked them
To tell the story one more time.

And yes, I did believe them
Though I'd not seen a thing.
I did not go to Bethlehem
Or hear the angels sing,
But there was something magic
   in the air
That made me feel as if I had
   been there.
I knew that as the world
Moves on through time,
There would be more stories just
   like mine
About the souls who've chosen
   to believe
In something that they never
   got to see.

Do you think you'll join us
Though you've not seen a thing?
You were not there in Bethlehem
To hear the angels sing.
But if you feel the spirit in the air,
Then, just like me, you'll know that
He was here . . . He was here.
The King of kings and Lord of
   lords was here,
He was here . . . He was here.
And He will come again, for
   He was here.

When the boy finished, he disappeared like sand in the wind. Isaac and Eliza turned to their elderly sitter, only to find that she was asleep on the couch.

"Should we wake her?" Eliza asked.

"Naw, let her sleep," Isaac said. He lowered his voice. "I wonder what else she's got in that backpack."

Before he could open the pack and peek inside, he heard a voice. "Just sandwiches—egg-salad sandwiches. Want some?" Isaac jumped and turned quickly, but the old woman's eyes were still tightly shut. A smile crept onto her face as she said: "It's a trick I learned working late nights in the nursery at the hospital. I could hold the babies, shut my eyes, rock 'em to sleep, and not miss a thing. Some call it a skill, but I think it's a gift . . . and I've got it."

A voice from inside the leather case shouted, "You learned that from me! I was doing that hundreds of years before you were even born."

"Better let Sarah out, Eliza." The sitter motioned to Eliza to open the case. When she did, a gust of wind blew into the room, and a beautiful woman in a long robe appeared. She was holding an ornament from the case, which she gave to Eliza. It was some swaddling cloth tied in the shape of a bow.

"Isaac, Eliza, this is Sarah. A very dear friend of mine," whispered the sitter. "She ran one of the greatest orphanages in ancient Israel and has a story I'd like her to tell you just the way she first told it to me."

Then the carpenter repeated
What he'd said so many times.
He said, "I was not His father;
    He was mine."
Then he humbly went on working
With his worn and calloused hands.
Though she did not ask more
    questions,
He knew she didn't understand.
And so he asked if she would
    help him.
He saw her answer in a glance.
And she did the chores he
    asked her,
And she was grateful for the chance.
Then they talked for hours of Jesus,
And how he knew He was divine.
He said, "I was not His father;
    He was mine.

How could one so foolish and so
    flawed
Ever hope to raise the Son of God?"
Then he spoke of the misgivings
He had had a thousand times,
And how Jesus found the tender
    moments
To let him know he'd done just fine.
Then the carpenter recited
The greatest truths he'd ever learned
And testified they came from Jesus.
And then her heart within her
    burned.
And they embraced as she departed,
Joseph told her one more time,
"Tell them I was not His father;
Tell them He was mine.
No, I was not His father;
    He was mine."

MARY LET ME HOLD
HER BABY

Mary let me hold her baby,
Her newborn son.
Though I'd never be a mother,
I felt like one.
Mary let me hold her baby
So she could rest.
And ever since that night I held Him,
My life's been blessed.
Those like me who can't have children
Still can be mothers.
Something in His eyes convinced me
I could serve so many others.
Mary let me hold her baby
So soft and warm.
Mary let me hold her baby,
And I was reborn.

As the music ended and the woman disappeared, the sitter said, "So, children, can I introduce you to the greatest egg-salad sandwiches in the world, or is there a limit to the number of Christmas miracles you can embrace in one night?" From her backpack the old woman pulled a sack filled with sandwiches. "You know," she said, "if you left Santa one of these sandwiches, he'd leave you any gift you ever wanted. They're that good."

"They might be," Isaac said sadly, "but some gifts even Santa can't give." He and Eliza sat down and began eating their sandwiches.

Don't tell me you've given up on Christmas miracles!" the sitter exclaimed. She opened her ornament case, took out what appeared to be a small manger, and placed it on the wreath.

"This one means the most to me," she said. "It's a cradle made by a carpenter for a newborn king. He loved Jesus before the baby was even born. I like to think that's how it was for my dad, who was overseas fighting for his country when my mom was pregnant with me. I believe he felt a little like Joseph did, wondering what it would be like to be a father, and that's why he wrote this carol."

JOSEPH
(I WAS NOT HIS FATHER, HE WAS MINE)

He was working late one evening
With the wood he knew so well,
When she thought she
 recognized him,
Though at first she couldn't tell.
As she humbly begged his pardon,
A strange sadness swelled inside
When she asked, "Aren't you
 the father
Of the man they crucified?"

You never met your father, did you?" Eliza asked.

The old woman didn't have to answer.

"You came to see us because you're like us," Isaac said. "You lost your father like we lost ours."

The sitter nodded softly and said, "But the difference between you and me, children, is that I'm not pretending to like Christmas. I love it. Know why? Because Christmas brings miracles that are much bigger than Christmas itself. They're more amazing than the people who came by to sing those Forgotten Carols for you tonight.

"You see, children, someone taught me, many years ago, that the miracles of Christmas are really just gifts to help us find faith in the greatest miracle of all."

"What's the greatest miracle of all?" Isaac asked breathlessly.

Oh, that's easy, my dear," said the sitter. "It's the gift you told me even Santa can't give. It may not come tonight," she whispered, touching the manger ornament gently, "but it will come."

She looked at the clock on the wall and sighed. "Time to say good night," she said, reaching to give each child a hug. "Good night, Isaac. Good night, Eliza."

Isaac said, "You know our names, but how do we say good night to you when we don't know yours?"

"Well, my name is Constance," she told them, smiling. "But all my friends call me Connie Lou."